THE LEGENDS OF KING ARTHUR
MERLIN, MAGIC AND DRAGONS

Dados Internacionais de Catalogação na Publicação (CIP) de acordo com ISBD

M469d   Mayhew, Tracey
        The dark sorceress / adaptado por Tracey Mayhew. – Jandira : W. Books, 2025.
        96 p. ; 12,8cm x 19,8cm. – (The legends of king Arthur)

        ISBN: 978-65-5294-163-3

        1. Literatura infantojuvenil. 2. Literatura Infantil. 3. Clássicos. 4. Literatura inglesa. 5. Lendas. 6. Folclore. 7. Mágica. 8. Cultura Popular. I. Título. II. Série.

2025-620   CDD 028.5
                                              CDU 82-93

Elaborado por Vagner Rodolfo da Silva - CRB-8/9410
Índice para catálogo sistemático:
1. Literatura infantojuvenil 028.5
2. Literatura infantojuvenil 82-93

The Legends of King Arthur: Merlin, Magic, and Dragons
Text © Sweet Cherry Publishing Limited, 2020
Inside illustrations © Sweet Cherry Publishing Limited, 2020
Cover illustrations © Sweet Cherry Publishing Limited, 2020

Text by Tracey Mayhew
Illustrations by Mike Phillips

© 2025 edition:
Ciranda Cultural Editora e Distribuidora Ltda.

1st edition in 2025
www.cirandacultural.com.br
No part of this publication may be reproduced, stored in a retrieval
system, or transmitted in any form or by any means, electronic,
mechanical, photocopying, recording, or otherwise, without written
permission of the publisher.
This book is a work of fiction. Names, characters, places, and incidents
are either the product of the author's imagination or are used fictitiously,
and any resemblance to actual persons, living or dead, business
establishments, events, or locales is entirely coincidental.

The Legends of King Arthur

The Dark Sorceress

Retold by
Tracey Mayhew

Illustrated by
Mike Phillips

Chapter One

Morgan thundered through the forest, her heart beating wildly in her chest. She could hear her father's hounds behind her. They sped through the undergrowth, closing in fast, their breathing

as ragged as hers.
She raced on
and didn't look
back. She knew they
would catch her, but
she was determined to run as fast and
as far as she could before they did.
Maybe she would even make it back to
Tintagel this time.

Leaping over a tree root, she
ducked beneath low hanging
branches, adrenaline coursing
through her veins. Finally, slowing
her pace, she dared to glance back.
Her dress caught instantly, making
her hit the ground hard.

The hounds were upon her. Morgan

barely stifled a giggle as they covered her face with drool, licking her enthusiastically.

'Get off me, Balor!' she laughed, pushing the large dog away. He snapped playfully at her. Glancing up at the darkening sky, Morgan knew the

time had come to return to Tintagel. Her mother would be expecting her.

'Come on then, you two. Let's go home.' She pushed herself to her feet and dusted off her dress.

The animals continued to play with each other. Despite being born from two of her father's favourite hunting hounds, Balor and Nera had never liked the sport. They preferred a warm spot by the fire to chasing hares and birds through the forest.

After a moment, Morgan whistled and the two hounds obediently came to heel. Together, they traced their way back to Tintagel.

As she walked, Morgan sighed, catching sight of the grass and mud stains on the maroon fabric of her skirts. Her mother would not be pleased that she had ruined yet another dress. She could almost hear her now:

'You're ten summers old, Morgan; far too grown-up to be running around the woods making a mess of yourself! Your place is here, learning to be a lady of the court.'

Morgan knew that she was not the type of girl her mother would have wanted. She was not dutiful like her older sisters, who were married and had families of their own, and she had no wish to spend all day sewing and practising singing. She knew her mother loved her dearly, but that didn't mean she wouldn't have preferred her to be more ladylike.

Stepping out of the trees, Morgan smiled at the sight of Tintagel. 'Race you back!' she challenged the hounds, sprinting ahead. They bounded after her, enjoying the unexpected game.

By the time they reached the castle, she was out of breath and coated in a layer of sweat. No, her mother would certainly not be pleased. Morgan smiled at the gatehouse guards as she passed, earning a quick nod in response, and made her way into the bustling courtyard.

'You've come back just in time, my lady,' Cerdic, one of the squires, called as he caught sight of her.

'What do you mean?' she asked, frowning at the older boy.

Cerdic nodded towards the castle. 'King Uther Pendragon's man is visiting your father–'

Morgan didn't wait to hear anything else. The king's man was there – at *Tintagel*! She knew that her father was a friend of the king, but he had always travelled to him; the king had never once sent anyone to them.

Morgan was determined to find out what was happening as she slipped through clusters of excited people. It wasn't long before she was making her way towards her father's receiving hall, where all of his guests were met. With no time to change her clothes, Morgan quickly ran her fingers through her hair before smoothing down her dress. It would not do to embarrass her father in front of the king's man.

As she reached the huge wooden door, the guards hesitated, giving her a brief once-over, before stepping aside. Morgan took a moment to compose herself.

That was when she heard it: a raised, angry voice coming from inside her father's receiving room.

Her *father's* voice.

'My lady, perhaps you should–'

Morgan shushed the guard, pressing her ear uselessly against the solid oak door. She frowned. Why was her father shouting?

'Get out!' her father bellowed furiously. 'The king insults me with this!'

Morgan scurried away from the door as hurried footsteps approached from the other side. She stepped into the shadows of the corridor just as the doors were thrown open and a man wearing the king's coat of arms marched out with his men.

Morgan watched as her father appeared in the doorway. He whispered to the guards, who immediately left and followed King Uther's men outside.

'Father?' She spoke quietly from the darkness, afraid of the look in her father's eyes. It was one she had never seen before.

Gorlois, Duke of Cornwall, looked at her. His eyes softened as he took in the sight of his youngest daughter.

'Morgan, what will your mother say when

she sees you?' he chuckled, his anger vanishing in an instant.

At that moment, what her mother would say was the furthest thing from Morgan's mind.

'Father, why were you shouting? Is everything alright?'

He sighed. 'Do not worry yourself, Morgan. The king will soon realise his mistake.' Holding out his arm, he gestured for her to approach.

With his arm around her, Morgan let him lead her into the receiving room, unable to ignore a nagging feeling. Despite her father's words, she knew that something was wrong.

Trouble was brewing at Tintagel.

Chapter Two

The next few days passed slowly at Tintagel. There was a strange kind of tension between her parents that had never been there before. Despite all her mother's attempts to get her father to talk, the duke would not.

It was hard for Morgan to see the sudden distance between parents who were usually so close. Her father would hide away in his study for hours, while her mother spent most of her time teaching sewing and music. As for Morgan, she would take Balor and Nera into the woods and spend most of her day there, running and chasing the dogs through the trees until they could barely stand.

Then the day came when a man from the king's court galloped into Tintagel. He carried a parchment with him.

'The king has declared war on us,' Morgan's father announced that night.

Fear made Morgan's blood run cold. *War!* She couldn't understand it. Why had the king declared war on her *father*? He was the king's friend. He had done nothing but serve the king loyally for many years. This made no sense.

But then she remembered the argument she had overheard, and realised that something terrible must have happened that day.

Looking at her father over the dinner table, Morgan saw the worry on his face. It scared her. She had never seen him so fearful before, so preoccupied. Her

mother looked no better as she watched her husband. His food and drink were untouched. Reaching out, Igraine covered the duke's hand with her own, offering him comfort that no one else could.

The rest of dinner was a quiet affair. After it, her father and his knights gathered in the war room, no doubt to talk about the upcoming battle.

Several weeks and a dozen skirmishes between her father's men and the king's passed. Days that Morgan spent with her mother, forbidden to leave the castle. She hated it. She felt trapped inside her own home, unable to escape for even a moment. But when she thought her life couldn't get any worse, her father told her the unthinkable: he was sending her away.

'Please, Father,' she sobbed, clutching at his arm. 'I won't leave you. I won't leave Mother …'

Her father looked down at her. His eyes were sympathetic but his answer was firm. 'Morgan, you cannot stay here. You need to be safe.'

'But *you* can keep me safe!' she insisted desperately. 'Just as you keep Mother safe!'

Her father smiled sadly, glancing at Igraine. 'I wish that I could,' he said quietly. 'But this place is no longer safe for a child. The king might lay siege.'

'But ...' Morgan looked to her mother for support, but all she could see was her own pain reflected back at her. Her mother was just as powerless to stop this as she was. 'Are you sending me to Elaine ... or Morgause?' she sniffed, hopeful that, although she was leaving her parents and her home, she might at least see her sisters.

The duke shook his head, sadly. 'A new life awaits you, Morgan. One your sisters never had.' He reached out, stroking her cheek. 'Leave here with your head held high, my love. And one day, when this war is over, you *shall* return to us.'

Knowing that it was hopeless to argue further, Morgan nodded. She hugged her father, before turning to her mother.

'Be brave, my child,' Igraine whispered as she hugged her.

Wiping her tears, Morgan stepped away from her parents and turned to the carriage that was waiting for her. As she climbed the steps, she knew that she was leaving everything she loved behind. She couldn't help wondering if she would ever see any of it again.

Chapter Three

Morgan had no idea where she was going, and on the rare occasion when the driver did stop, he would barely acknowledge her questions.

All she knew was that the journey was long and hard. The carriage rattled over rough, uneven ground for what seemed like days, bouncing Morgan around on the hard wooden seat, leaving her with a pounding headache and an aching back. Eventually night closed in and she could no longer see outside.

Morgan sighed as she pulled her furs tighter around her. Slumping back on her uncomfortable seat, she finally allowed herself to think of her parents. What were they doing now? Were they together, or was her father locked up in his war room planning another

battle against the king? Or worse still, was he camped out in the middle of a battlefield, unsure if he would make it back to Tintagel alive?

She sat up as the movement of the carriage changed, the wheels crunching over gravel now. Peering out, Morgan searched the darkness for any sign of where she was but could see nothing.

Finally, the carriage slowed and came to a stop. Morgan threw the door open, leaping to the ground without waiting for the steps to be lowered. She froze when she caught sight of the three nuns standing before her.

Nuns!

She had been brought to a *nunnery*!

Morgan stared at the severe-looking women, their faces shadowed by their habits. They were as still and silent as statues, looking back at her.

After a moment, Morgan's gaze shifted to the building behind them. The full moon lit up the looming towers but cast the rest in darkness.

The tallest nun stepped forwards, her small eyes watching Morgan carefully. 'I am Mother Edith,' she declared in a hard voice. She indicated the two nuns standing behind her. 'This is Sister Hilda and Sister Mildrith.' The two nuns bowed their heads, their hands clasped before them.

Unsure of what to say, Morgan shifted from one foot to the other. Hesitantly, she began, 'I … I am Lady Morgan, daughter of Duke Gorlois of Cornwall.'

Mother Edith barely acknowledged her words. 'Iona will show you to your chamber,' she announced. 'She will be your teacher whilst you are here.'

Looking around, Morgan frowned and was about to ask who Iona was, when a lady stepped from the shadows. If Morgan had thought that Mother Edith was severe, Iona was absolutely terrifying. She was tall, far taller than any lady Morgan had ever seen. Her dark eyes seemed to bore into Morgan,

searching for her deepest secrets.
Iona's white hair was pulled back into
a tight bun, a stark contrast to the
black robes she wore.

'Come,' she instructed as she turned away, towards the nunnery.

Morgan scurried after her, leaving the driver to follow with her bag. 'Are you a nun?' Morgan asked as soon as she caught up.

'What I am does not matter,' Iona muttered. 'What matters is what you are, child.'

'I don't understand ...'

Iona glanced down at her. 'You will ... in time.'

Morgan frowned at the strange reply, but said nothing as she continued to follow Iona through a dark doorway and into a candlelit maze of corridors. Finally, they stopped outside a heavy oak door.

'You will join the other girls at breakfast in the morning,' Iona informed her. 'One of them will knock for you.' Then she turned away, retracing her steps.

Teeming with questions, but too exhausted to pursue either them or Iona, Morgan pushed open the heavy door and stepped inside. The chamber was bare except for a bed and a wooden chair in one corner. It was a far cry from the familiar luxuries of her own room, though she had never been a girl who prized finery.

Morgan sighed as the driver deposited her bag on the stone floor. 'Will you tell Mother and Father that I love them and miss them?' she asked, feeling her throat tighten.

The man bowed. 'Of course, my lady.' He

glanced around the cheerless chamber, before turning back to Morgan. 'Be safe, my child,' he added softly.

And with that, he was gone, leaving Morgan alone.

Throwing herself onto the hard bed, Morgan finally gave in to heartache and homesickness, sobbing uncontrollably, until sleep finally claimed her.

Chapter Four

For the next few days, Morgan waited for word from her father that the war was over and that she could safely return home. But the days turned to weeks and the weeks to months. Finally, whole years crawled by.

With her noble background, Morgan could have spent her time with the nuns on spinning and embroidery. But even if she'd had the talent, she lacked the will. And she had ruined so many manuscripts in her attempts to decorate their borders that she was banned from that particular chore altogether.

Morgan still preferred to be outside anyway, and cared little for how the harder work of growing vegetables and grain made her hands rough and unladylike. Besides, the nuns all swore that the bees produced more honey under Morgan's charge than any other's.

In all this time, Morgan had received only a few letters from her mother and sisters. None of them told her anything about how the war was going, only that it still raged. So she lived every day praying for news, while at the same time dreading it. Dreading that one day, one letter, would bring news of the worst possible kind.

And that letter eventually came.

Her father had been killed in battle.

Morgan stared at the parchment in her hands, numb to everything around her. He was dead, killed by the man who had waged war against him for so long, for no reason she had ever been told.

King Uther Pendragon.

The name ignited a fire within her, a storm that had been building for eight summers now. Something dark rose up as if it would carry her with it–

'Morgan!'

The sharpness in Iona's voice pulled Morgan's attention from the letter to the door where her teacher stood, watching her carefully.

'I'm sorry, Mistress,' she muttered.

Iona stepped forwards, closing the door behind her. 'We've talked about this, Morgan,' she said. 'No matter what, you cannot let your emotions get the better of you.'

Morgan nodded, knowing that she was right. Ever since she had turned thirteen, strange things had been happening to her. At first they had been harmless, like reviving a dying plant with her hands, or helping to heal minor illnesses in the infirmary.

But there had been other times too. Times when she was angry or upset, when her "energy", as Iona insisted on calling it, had got the better of her, and more sinister things had happened. Once, when one of the novices had upset her, Morgan had caused the girl to fall without even being near her.

To have such power both scared and fascinated Morgan.

Sensing the strength of her untrained abilities, Iona had taken Morgan aside and begun teaching her how to control her emotions so that she wouldn't cause any more accidents. So far these extra lessons had been going well.

Glancing at the letter once more, Morgan reread her mother's words:

I bring you grave news, my child. Your father has been killed in battle ... He is dead ...

'What is it?' Iona asked, her eyes searching Morgan's face. 'Speak.'

'My father …' For a moment, Iona's eyes softened, but before she could speak, Morgan turned away. The last thing she wanted was pity.

Iona reached out. 'My child, you are at a crossroads–'

Morgan shook her head, not wanting to hear this right now. 'Leave me.' Iona took another step towards Morgan. Rounding on the older woman, Morgan growled, anger boiling inside her. '*Leave me,*' she hissed.

'Morgan, listen to me,' Iona insisted.
But Morgan was in no mood to
listen. 'I said *leave!*' Slashing her arm
through the air released a bolt of white
light, missing Iona by inches. Part of
the stone wall exploded behind her.
Staring at her own hand, Morgan was
shocked into stillness.

Nevertheless, the older woman made no further move to approach her. 'You cannot ignore me, Morgan. You cannot ignore your powers any longer;

they are *too* strong.' Iona was firm, unyielding. 'You are one of the fay. We need to talk about what is happening to you.' The fay, as Iona had explained in her teachings, were women with the power to cast spells.

'Not now,' Morgan insisted, sparks still dancing around her fingertips. She almost smiled to herself. A part of her was beginning to enjoy this power.

Iona nodded. 'Soon,' she promised ominously.

With a flick of her wrist, Morgan slammed the heavy door shut behind her teacher as she left.

She knew Iona was right; they did need to talk. Every day, Morgan felt herself changing. Her powers, whatever they were, were changing her. She had to deal with them.

But not today.

Today she would grieve for her father.

Chapter Five

Every day Iona taught Morgan more about healing and herbal remedies, but she was now also teaching her about darker things. She would not only explain the benefits of certain plants, but the dangers as well. She wanted Morgan to understand what would happen if too much of one herb was added to a man's drink, what affect it would have on him, how much pain it would cause and for how long.

Every night Morgan retreated to her chamber, with nothing but thoughts of her father till morning. Had he suffered at the hands of his enemy? Had Uther looked him in the eye as he drove his sword into him? Had he watched the life drain from her father's eyes with triumph?

And still her mother's letter went unanswered. Morgan wanted to reach out, to seek comfort and to offer comfort in return, but she didn't know how. What could she say when she was so consumed with thoughts of hatred and revenge?

It was almost a month later when another letter arrived. Nothing could have prepared Morgan for what it contained.

Her mother was to be married.

To *Uther Pendragon.*

Indeed, she was already pregnant with his child.

Seeing those words, written so clearly, in her mother's own hand,

Morgan felt rage like no other. She couldn't have controlled it even if she had wanted to.

White light danced around her fingertips, setting the parchment ablaze, fire ripping through Igraine's words.

Before she knew what she was doing, Morgan found herself standing outside Iona's door. Her mother's words, her mother's *actions*, had made up her mind for her.

The door opened without her knocking. 'At last,' Iona murmured.

Morgan lowered her hand. 'You knew I was coming?'

Iona merely smiled.

'You have dark powers, don't you? Powers like mine?'

Iona nodded.

'I want you to teach me everything you know,' Morgan declared.

Iona studied her for a long moment before speaking. 'The line you walk is a dangerous one, Morgan. The balance between light and dark is delicate. Once you cross it, you can never go back.'

Thoughts of Uther Pendragon and her mother filled Morgan's head. Images of her father's body ...

'I have no wish to go back,' she stated coldly.

Iona looked satisfied. 'Then our new lessons begin tomorrow.'

Chapter Six

Morgan learnt all that she could from Iona. She learnt how to mix the deadliest of potions, how to transform into something, or someone, else. Most importantly, she learnt how to control her emotions so that she wouldn't accidentally reveal her powers to the world. Her favourite lesson by far was learning to control the elements. To have so much power was exciting!

'You burn with such hatred, Morgan,' Iona told her during one lesson. 'You must learn to control yourself. Do not let it consume you because that is when your enemies will win.'

Losing to Uther Pendragon was out of the question, and the very idea made Morgan more determined than ever to master her powers.

Her greatest test came, as the last one had, with a letter. Her mother's wedding had taken place.

Morgan's time had come.

Quickly writing a reply, Morgan apologised for her silence since her father's death.

Sorrow must be her excuse. She would, of course, come and visit the happy couple to celebrate their marriage. Igraine was only too pleased to welcome her daughter back to Tintagel, where she and Uther were staying until the birth.

Knowing that Uther Pendragon was staying at Tintagel, her father's home, only angered Morgan more. Could her mother not see how wrong that was? Or did she no longer care? Was her new husband, her new baby, all that mattered to her now?

Returning to Tintagel was harder than Morgan had imagined it would be. There was no rush of dogs to greet her, and there were few faces that she recognised. Seeing her mother so happy, standing so proudly beside the king in what had once been the duke's receiving room, broke Morgan's heart still further. She wanted to shake her mother. She wanted to demand how she could dishonour the memory of her father like this.

Instead she smiled and curtsied and played the dutiful daughter. Even as Uther welcomed her to Tintagel like a guest in her own home. As he stood smiling at her through his neatly trimmed beard, Morgan fought the urge to scream that Tintagel had been hers long before it was his.

'I trust your journey was good?' Uther asked.

'Very good, Your Majesty,' she assured him.

'Good, good. Your mother has missed you terribly.'

Morgan nodded, forcing herself to smile at her mother. 'I've missed her, too.'

For a moment, it felt right to let her mother take her hand. It felt like it always had. Like Igraine would protect her from anything. But Morgan knew that was no longer true: Igraine had betrayed her, betrayed her father.

'I'm so happy you've come home,' Igraine smiled, her free hand stroking her belly.

Home ...

Looking around, Morgan knew that this place was no longer her home. Although it still bustled with people, it felt empty somehow. Her father's spirit ... gone.

Uther's attention was drawn from Morgan by a movement behind her. A man had entered the receiving room. He was tall and wore black robes that matched the colour of his hair.

'Your Majesty.' He bowed, stopping before the king.

'Ah, Morgan, I'd like you to meet Merlin, my good friend and advisor,' Uther

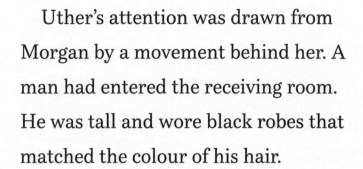

announced proudly. 'There's not a man I trust more.'

Morgan met Merlin's unreadable gaze and knew, instantly, that he would be a problem. Something about him worried her, although she couldn't say what. He looked only a few years older than Morgan, but she had the feeling that he was far older.

'Good day, my lady,' Merlin said, bowing his head respectfully.

Morgan curtsied. 'Good day.'

Raising his eyes, Merlin held her gaze for a moment, before turning his attention back to the king. 'Sire, may I speak with you? It is a matter of great importance.'

The king nodded. 'Of course.'
Turning to Igraine, Uther smiled.
'I shall see you at dinner, my love.'
He placed a tender kiss on her cheek.
Morgan had to look away.

'Let me show you where the baby
will have his cradle,' Igraine began,
after the king had led Merlin from
the room.

'*His* cradle?' Morgan asked.

Igraine laughed. 'Uther is certain
it will be a boy,' she explained,
smiling fondly.

Morgan nodded, trying to take this
in. If the baby were a boy, it would
mean that he would inherit everything
that belonged to his father upon King

Uther's death. It would mean that Tintagel would be his.

Morgan would be left with nothing.

No. She wouldn't let that happen.

Igraine took to her bed a few weeks later, her pregnancy almost at an end. Morgan tried desperately to avoid her. The last thing she wanted was to witness the birth of a half-brother destined to take everything that had once been hers.

But hearing her mother's cries pulled Morgan to her side, and she was soon helping her through the birth, easing her pain with herbs and potions.

It wasn't long before the shrill sounds of a baby's cry filled the room.

'It's a boy, my queen,' the doctor announced, standing up and showing her the newborn.

Morgan felt her heart stop: *a boy*. She watched the doctor wrap the baby in linen before handing him to his mother, who gazed down at him lovingly. 'Oh, Morgan. Uther was right! It's a boy. A beautiful baby boy!' She looked up at her daughter, happiness shining in her eyes. 'Isn't he beautiful? His name will be Arthur, as Uther decreed.'

Morgan swallowed, unable to speak. This was what she had dreaded. 'I'll help them clean up ...' she muttered, picking up the nearest bowl as she hurried from the room.

Once outside, she leant against the wall, knowing that she could not wait any longer.

Chapter Seven

'He's gone, Morgan!' Igraine wailed, when Morgan visited her the following morning.

'Who's gone?' Morgan asked, hoping that she was talking about Uther. Glancing around the room, she noticed that the baby's cradle was empty. Even the embroidered linens were gone.

'Arthur!' Igraine sobbed, covering her face with her hands and curling up into a ball on the bed.

Morgan approached. 'What do you mean he's gone? Where?' Her

heartbeat quickened as she scanned the chamber again, expecting to see the baby this time.

'We don't know! M-Merlin told Uther he would be safe this way!'

The name of Uther's friend brought Morgan's attention back to her mother. '*Merlin* took him? Why would he do that?'

'He said a dark storm was gathering over Tintagel.' Igraine wiped away tears. 'He said the baby could only survive it if we let him take him away. Let him be hidden somewhere no one would ever find him.' She sat up abruptly, wrapping her arms around herself. 'I'm sorry. I shouldn't have told you that. Uther said it must remain our secret.'

Morgan placed a hand on her mother's shoulder. 'I shall keep your secret, Mother,' she promised quietly. 'I shall say nothing of this.'

And she meant it. After all, it would not suit her plan.

Looking up at her, Igraine smiled through fresh tears. 'Thank you, Morgan. Thank you. I'm so glad you're here.'

With her mother still confined to bed, Morgan knew that this was her chance. Merlin was gone and Uther was preoccupied with grief – she would have no better opportunity for revenge.

Uther barely spoke a word to her at dinner, and no one else had been invited to join them at the table. Morgan watched as he drank cup after cup of wine. Cup after cup of the poison she had mixed earlier that day, with Iona's instructions in her head.

All Morgan had to do now was wait.

As Uther stumbled to his bedchamber, Morgan went to her own. In the silence of the night, she called upon her powers of transformation.

Picturing her mother's face in her mind, her fairer hair, her fuller figure, Morgan's power

surged. As the feeling of warmth faded, she reached out, passing a hand over a nearby candle and bringing the flame to life. Picking up a looking glass, she smiled at her reflection; Igraine's face smiled back.

Quietly leaving her chamber, Morgan made her way through the shadowed halls, avoiding the guards, until she reached a faded tapestry in a neglected corner. She stroked the threads of forest leaves and hunting dogs. Her heart softened remembering Balor and Nera. She hardened it, and swept the tapestry aside.

Tintagel had many secret passageways, but only one that led to the king's own bedchamber. A secret Morgan knew, because it had once been her father's bedchamber.

The narrow passageway was stale and cobwebbed, as if Morgan had been the last to use it. It felt even smaller in the body of an adult, and she no longer needed a candle to guide her. Instead Morgan summoned a single flame

in the palm of her hand, and picked her way across the uneven stones. Finally she slipped into a well-lit room. It was more grandly furnished than she remembered it. The king was on the floor, groaning in pain, covered in sweat.

She had chosen something slow and painful for him.

Morgan extinguished the flame in her hand. Hearing noise from the

far corner, Uther opened his eyes and found himself looking at his wife. 'My love,' he begged, 'help me. Something is wrong.' "Igraine" made no move to come closer. She simply continued to stare down at him.

'Igraine? What–?' He cried out in pain. 'Help me, *please*!'

She stepped forwards then, and as Morgan allowed her power to fade, her own face was revealed. Uther cried out in shock and confusion. '*You!*' Reaching out, he clutched her ankle. 'Please ... help me. I beg you!'

Shaking his hand off, Morgan crouched just out of reach. 'You took my father's life,' she reminded him

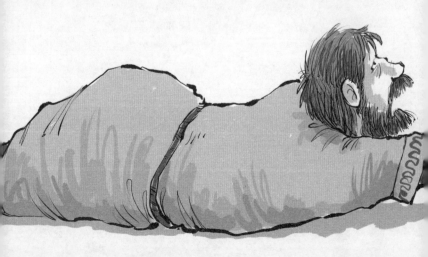

coldly. 'Your war cost me everything. Now you must answer for it.' She gazed at him, knowing that he had already lost the strength to fight. 'Now *I* shall take everything from *you*. And I promise you, Uther Pendragon, that I include your son in that.

I *will* find Arthur, and when I do the Pendragon name will be no more.'

Hearing this, in a last, desperate effort, Uther summoned his strength and made a grab for Morgan's arm ...

But it was too late.

Looking down at the king's lifeless body, Morgan stood, letting her anger flow. White light crackled at her fingertips, thunder rumbled through the night.

Her life was not supposed to be this way. She had been a happy child, content to pass her days at Tintagel, sewing poorly and playing with dogs. Her parents had not raised her to feel this hatred, but circumstances had twisted her into someone she didn't recognise anymore.

Her life had taken a very different path from the one she had been born to follow. Now here she was, in the place that had once held so many happy memories, her revenge almost complete ...

Almost, but not quite.

She had lost the boy.

Tearing her gaze from the king's body, Morgan scanned the room,

recalling better times. This was the place where she had sat with her father, listening to stories of knights and princesses. A place she had loved.

But those times were long gone, and Morgan was no princess. This place was one of heartache now: her own and her father's. Morgan was only grateful that he never knew his wife's betrayal. But she did. And it was only a matter of time before Arthur paid the same price as his father.

Morgan rode a stolen horse from Tintagel that night, her mother's fresh screams of despair issuing in her wake. She stopped only once, to say a final, silent farewell to her father, and to the girl she had once been.

She had returned to Tintagel as Lady Morgan, daughter of Gorlois, Duke of Cornwall.

She was leaving as Morgan le Fay: the dark sorceress.

Continue the quest with the next book in the series!

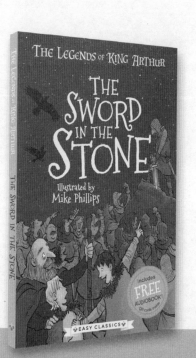
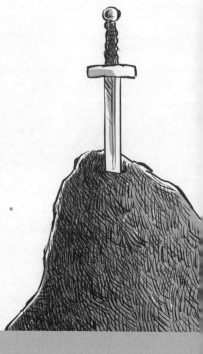

"This series opens the door to a treasure house of wonderful stories which have previously been available chiefly to older readers. We can only welcome it as a fabulous resource for all who love magical tales, and those who will come to love them."

John Matthews
Author of the Red Dragon Rising series and Arthur of Albion